THE AI

ROBERT L BUTLER JR

www.dizzyemupublishing.com

DIZZY EMU PUBLISHING

1714 N McCadden Place, Hollywood, Los Angeles 90028

www.dizzyemupublishing.com

The Alliance

Robert L Butler Jr

ISBN: 9781795760539

First published in the United States

in 2019 by Dizzy Emu Publishing

www.dizzyemupublishing.com

THE ALLIANCE

ROBERT L BUTLER JR

The Alliance

By

Robert L Butler Jr

Based on the story/characters created by Robert L Butler Jr
July 2018

July 2018   rlb-jr@comcast.net
                             253-250-7848

1 INT- OFFICE BLDG- DAY

Man outside a office door standing guard. Inside room there
is a man counting money,this man is Smooth,member of the
Alliance,with him is his bodyguard Mitch,while counting
money he hears a noise outside the door. He closes brief
case, Mitch goes to the door, the door opens,and 3 men walk
thru the door. Just as Mitch reaches for his gun,the 2 men
pull their guns out and shake their heads. The other man,is
Danny,he walks toward Smooth and hands him a cell
phone,phone begins to ring,Smooth looks at it

                    DANNY
          well it's not for me

Smooth lets the phone ring a few times,then answers. On the
phone is a gangster known as Big Uce

                    SMOOTH
          WHO THE FUCK IS THIS?

                    BIG UCE
          That's not the question you should
          be asking

                    SMOOTH
          Oh really

                    BIG UCE
          you should be asking..,How do I
          know who you are? and ..what do you
          want to be?

                    SMOOTH
          The fuck you mean,what do I want to
          be?

                    BIG UCE
          you want to be a rich man...or a
          dead man!

Smooth thinking,and looking at the men in front of him,men
with the guns are itching to pull the trigger,he looks at
Mitch,Danny has a slight grin on his face

                    SMOOTH
          I want to be rich

                    BIG UCE
          good boy!

Big Uce hangs up phone. Danny motions to Smooth to give him
the phone. Smooth tosses it to him. The men lower their guns

                                        (CONTINUED)

                      DANNY
            Here is the deal..you will be in
            charge of distribution of our
            product effective immediately..your
            cut will be 40%

                      SMOOTH
            40%? That's only 10 when I split it
            with-

                      DANNY
            I think you are confused! You have
            one partner now..you were just
            talking to him..and don't worry
            about your former partners,they
            will be dealt with

Smooth frowns in disbelief

                      SMOOTH
            But-

                      DANNY
             -We will be in touch!

The men walk out of the room. Smooth sits down in his
chair,pondering what has just happened, Mitch runs to the
door,and opens it and see's his guard laying on the floor
dead. He looks left then right then shuts door.

                              FADE TO

                         OPENING CREDITS

2 INT-MIKE HOUSE-DAY

Man in his living room,playing video games. He checks his
watch,stop playing the game and gets up. Goes in safe,gets
his gun. This is Mike,member of the Alliance, he
then heads to the kitchen

3 INT-MIKE'S KITCHEN-DAY

Mike's wife is cooking food,he comes up behind hugs her they
kiss.

Mike exits the house

                              CUT TO

4 EXT-MIKE HOUSE-DAY

Mike is headed to his car. He opens the driver side door
gets in,he puts the keys in the ignition,starts up his car
and from the back seat ,Jace wearing a mask appears behind
him and strangles Mike, killing him.

Jace exits the vehicle from the back and heads toward the
house.

Jace at Mikes door,slowly puts key in lock and slowly opens
the front door

                                                    CUT TO

5 INT-MIKE'S HOUSE - DAY

Jace enters the house ,slowly closes the door,he see's Mikes
wife in the kitchen,her back is facing him. He slowly walks
toward her. Then he raises his arm,and is holding a gun with
silencer on it. Mike's wife still cooking,then turns
around,she turns on the faucet then looks up,and see's the
mask man and before she can scream,he fires a shot hitting
her in the head instantly. she falls to the floor. He heads
to the kitchen,fires 3 more shots into her,then heads for
the front door,but stops and see's a crib ,looks in the
crib,see's a baby sleep,then fires a shot killing the baby.

Jace headed for the front door,then hears kids playing up
stairs, he re-loads his gun then he slowly heads up stairs

                                                    CUT TO

6 INT-MIKES HOUSE UPSTAIRS-DAY

Jace upstairs,slowly walking gets to the room where the kids
are playing opens the door,the 2 boys don't notice him,he
shoots them both.

                                                    FADE TO

7 INT-SMOOTH HOUSE -EVE

Smooth sitting on the couch watching t.v with his
daughter,he is in deep thought not really watching,while his
wife is in kitchen fixing dinner. Cell phone rings, Smooth
picks it up

                                                (CONTINUED)

                    SMOOTH
          Yeah

                    BIG UCE
          you watching the news right now?

Smooth picks up the remote turns to the news.

                    NEWS REPORTER
          a family of 5 was found dead in
          this Lakewood apartment complex,
          The husband was found strangled to
          death in his car,while his wife and
          kids were shot to death execution
          style-

Smooth turns off t.v.

                    BIG UCE
          One down..two to go!

Smooth hangs up.Smooth slowly lowers his cell phone,has a
blank stare on his face,his daughter is tapping him on the
leg, he is looking at her,but not acknowledging her.
Daughter is talking but Smooth can't hear her,then her voice
begins to get louder

                    DAUGHTER
          Daddy...Daddy!

                    SMOOTH
          uh..yeah baby..what is it

                    DAUGHTER
          dinner is ready

His daughter leaves to eat. Smooth picks up his phone and
dials

                    SMOOTH
          Tell the fellas we need to meet
          tomorrow night..JUST DO IT!

Smooth hangs up the phone,sits on the couch with a blank
stare on his face

                                        FADE TO

8 EXT-BALCONY- DAY

Photographer is snapping pictures of a famous model
,Anastasia, in different poses. Room is filled with a few
people, make up girl,and the models manager and a few grips.

                                                    CUT TO

9 INT-HOUSE -DAY

Man walking up the stairs. This man is Breeze a member of
the Alliance. He stops at a door and looks outside at the
photo shot. His cell phone rings he raises it to his ear.

                                                    CUT TO

10 EXT-BALCONY -DAY

Photo shoot is done. Grips start packing up the lights.

                         ROBB
                OK,that's a wrap

                         ANASTASIA
                finally

Anastasia goes and sits in her chair to get her make up
taken off. Her manager walks over to talk to her

                         SONJA
                OK we are done for the day. so
                tomorrow our flight for New york
                leaves at 10 am.

While they are talking,Breeze cones thru the door, Anastasia
sees him, gets up and goes over to him. They hug

                         ANASTASIA
                I was wondering if you would show
                up

                         BREEZE
                I told you I would come

Breeze hands her a rose

                         ANASTASIA
                awww your so sweet,thank you

Anastasia smells the rose and turns around and walks to the
ledge and looks out at the view of the water,Breeze comes up
behind her and hugs her

                                            (CONTINUED)

                         ANASTASIA
              I love this view,it reminds so much
              of home

                         BREEZE
              yes it is beautiful,

Anastasia turns around and faces Breeze,

                         BREEZE
              but not as beautiful as you

Anastasia blushes and Breeze gentle caresses her face,pulls
her close,they kiss

                         BREEZE
              so,you want to grab a bite to eat?

                         ANASTASIA
              yes!, I'm starving!

                         BREEZE
              so what do you want a salad?
              (laughing)

                         ANASTASIA
              Hell No! I been dieting all week, I
              want a big fat juicy steak,and some
              steak fries, and a banana split for
              dessert!

                         BREEZE
              Dam! you gonna eat all that?

                         ANASTASIA
              watch me, let me go get changed.

Anastasia kisses him on the check and turns to leave,then
turns back around

                         ANASTASIA
              is there a place around here where
              we can eat and still enjoy this
              view?

                         BREEZE
              yeah, I know the perfect place

Anastasia leaves to get dressed, Breeze pulls out his cell
phone

                         BREEZE
                Yeah,I want to make a reservation

                                                        CUT TO

11 INT-RESTAURANT-EVENING

Breeze and Anastasia sitting at table,they are finished
eating dinner. Waitress is re-filling their glasses,
waitress leaves.

They toast and drink,and both look at the view of the water.
Then they both look back at each other, they begin to hold
hands and smile and stare at each other for a bit.

Waitress comes back

                         TAMMY
                can I get you folks anything else?
                dessert maybe?

                         ANASTASIA
                yes I would like a banana split

                         TAMMY
                and for you sir

                         BREEZE
                I'm fine thank you

                         TAMMY
                I'll get that order in for you
                ma'am

                         ANASTASIA
                Thank you,oh and where is the
                ladies room

                         TAMMY
                just follow me ma'am, right this
                way

Anastasia and Tammy leave. Breeze looking out at the
ocean,takes a sip of his drink,his cell phone rings.

                         BREEZE
                hello..what? wait..slow down..what
                the?

Breeze gets up from the table,pacing back and forth while on
the phone, he see's Anastasia coming back,and heads back to
the table

                                                      (CONTINUED)

                         BREEZE
              I'll hit you back in an hour

Breeze hangs up his cell phone. Anastasia sits back down.
Breeze sits back down

                         BREEZE
              I got some bad news baby,I'm not
              going to be able to stay with you
              tonight

                         ANASTASIA
              But its my last night here

                         BREEZE
              I know baby..I am sorry..but
              something came up

                         ANASTASIA
              But when will I see you again? I
              wont be back here for a couple of
              months

                         BREEZE
              Tell you what,I'll dip into my
              savings,and next month I will visit
              you in Chicago..OK?

                         ANASTASIA
                   (pouting)
              OK...

Breeze summons the waitress.

                         BREEZE
              can you bring the check please?

                         ANASTASIA
              what about my dessert?

                         BREEZE
              can you make that to go

                         TAMMY
              yes sir

                                              CUT TO

12 EXT-HOUSE -EVE

Breeze walking Anastasia to her door. They get to the door
she turns and faces him.

                    BREEZE
          have a safe trip OK?

They kiss and hug,she turns to go inside

                    BREEZE
          I'll see you in Chicago

                    ANASTASIA
          you promise?

                    BREEZE
          I promise

Anastasia has a big smile on her face,she goes inside and
shuts the door.

                                        CUT TO

13 INT-CONFERENCE ROOM- EVENING

Smooth and Breeze are sitting at a table with his bodyguard
Steve standing up behind him. Mitch is standing behind
Smooth

                    BREEZE
          MIKE IS DEAD!

                    SMOOTH
          somebody killed him and his family

                    BREEZE
          WHERE THE FUCK WAS HIS BOYS?

                    MITCH
          it was Sunday

                    BREEZE
          SO! WHAT THE FUCK THAT DOES THAT
          SUPPOSE TO MEAN!

                    MITCH
           Sunday truce been around
          forever..nobody does any dirt that
          day...

                                        (CONTINUED)

                              BREEZE
                    except for the mother fucker that
                    killed Mike!

                              SMOOTH
                    look!..we can't be sure Mike's
                    death was a hit or not..he had lots
                    of enemies,shit we all do.. and
                    that crazy ass baby momma he
                    had,what's her name? shit, the game
                    is the game

Breeze and his bodyguard Steve look at each other,then
Breeze looks back at Smooth

                              BREEZE
                    Really? the game is the game
                    huh..That was a mother fucking hit!
                    baby mommas don't do shit like
                    that! I don't care how crazy they
                    are!

                              SMOOTH
                    look..all I'm saying is since we
                    formed this alliance...we haven't
                    had any problems for the last 20
                    years.. so if it was a hit,and I'm
                    not saying wasn't,we will deal with
                    it! But,in the mean time we beef up
                    security,watch our backs but,
                    business must go on!

                              BREEZE
                         (sarcastically)
                    business must go on huh?? speaking
                    of business..where the fuck Vince?

                              SMOOTH
                    No shit..(to Mitch) Call Vince
                    again

Mitch takes out his cell phone.

                                                        CUT TO

14 EXT- VINCE HOUSE- EVENING

                                                        CUT TO

15 INT-VINCE HOUSE LIVING ROOM- EVENING

Vince,member of the alliance is on the couch with his
wife,he hands her a birthday card.

Shew reads the card,hugs him,his cell phone rings,he answers

                    VINCE
          what's up? no, no ,no, it's my
          wife's birthday!. what?..really?
          alright I'll be there in about 30
          minutes

Vince hangs up cell, Sheri looking at him very upset
          HELL NO! Today of all days! YOU
          PROMISED!

                    VINCE
          Baby,I'm sorry,some shit went down
          and I got to-

Door bell rings,Vince smiles

                    SHERI
          and you got to what?

                    VINCE
          I got to handle something,but in
          the meantime,you need to get the
          door

Doorbell rings again

                    SHERI
          why?

                    VINCE
          just get the door

Wife gets up to answer the door,still mad

                    SHERI
          you not off the hook yet! we gonna
          finish this conversation

16 INT-FRONT DOOR- EVENING

She opens the door and there is a man standing in door way
with bunch of balloons that read Happy Birthday.

She smiles and takes the balloons and turns back to talk to
Vince.

(CONTINUED)

Man with the balloons slowly reaches behind his back for
something

                         SHERI
           This is nice but I am still mad-

She turns back toward the man there is a gun pointed in her
face,it's Jace,before she can scream, he shoots her,she
drops instantly to the floor.

Jace closes the door and heads inside the house.

                                                 CUT TO

17 INT-LIVING ROOM-EVENING

Vince on the couch waiting for his wife to come back,hears
what he thinks is her coming down the hall

                         VINCE
           so did you like the-

Vince looks up and see's a man standing in hall way.

                         VINCE
           who the fuck are you?

Vince starts to get up,Jace raises his arm up shoots
Vince,Vince falls back on the couch,Jace walks over to Vince
and fires 4 shots into his head, killing him.

                                                 CUT TO

18 INT-CONFERENCE ROOM- EVENING

                         MITCH
                    (hanging up phone)
           He said he will be here in 30
           minutes.

                         SMOOTH
           OK, in the mean time, Breeze..I
           need you to do me a favor.

Smooth motions to Breeze for him to come sit closer to him.
Breeze with a puzzled look on his face,looks back at
Steve,gets up and goes over and sits next to him.

                         SMOOTH
           I need you to handle the next
           shipment

                                            (CONTINUED)

                              BREEZE
              me! why me?..and why you acting
              like you in charge and giving out
              orders and shit!

                              SMOOTH
              look ,I'm not giving out orders,
              Mike use to take care of it..now
              that he is dead, I just figured-

                              MITCH
              I'll take care of it

                              SMOOTH
              I don't think so!

                              MITCH
              Boss..all I'm saying is-

                              SMOOTH
              hold up! Last time I checked,you
              was muscle right?...muscle aint got
              no mouth! muscle aint got no brain!
              muscle just follows orders!

Smooth Standing up,staring at Mitch,Mitch head down,feeling
embarrassed,not looking at Smooth

                              BREEZE
              Bro, you need us to step out while
              you handle your business?

Mitch, head down still down,Smooth still staring at him,
Steve and Breeze look at each other ,trying not to
laugh,Smooth then calms down,then sits down.

                              SMOOTH
              I was just thinking about what you
              said,somebody should have been
              there to have Mike's back..but we
              will deal with that soon..so can
              you handle the drop tonight? its
              for your territory.

Breeze looking at Smooth,then looks at Steve, and thinking,
Smooth reaches under the table and grabs a briefcase and
puts it on the table.

                              SMOOTH
              Come on bro,what would Jesus do?

Breeze looks back as Steve,the both have shocked looks on
their faces

>   BREEZE
>   (chuckles)
>   what?

>   SMOOTH
>   I'm saying,in this situation what
>   would Jesus do?

>   BREEZE
>   you talking about Jesus that owns
>   the car wash?

>   SMOOTH
>   Naw bro, Jesus (looks up to the
>   sky), what would Jesus do?

Breeze looks back as Steve ,Steve shakes his head,trying not
to laugh, Breeze thinks for a moment

>   BREEZE
>   well first of all, I don't think
>   that the son of god,that was out
>   there performing miracles, like
>   turning water to wine,would be
>   selling coke on the streets!

>   SMOOTH
>   shit..you never know

They both laugh,then Smooth unlocks the briefcase and slides
it over to Breeze. Breeze opens it.

>   BREEZE
>   How much is in here

>   SMOOTH
>   500 thousand

>   BREEZE
>   I don't think so

He slides the briefcase around to face Smooth, Smooth looks
inside

>   SMOOTH
>   Shit!

Smooth closes the briefcase,hands it to Mitch

>   SMOOTH
>   Go tell James,the count is wrong

Mitch takes the briefcase,heads out the room,Breeze signals
to Steve to follow Mitch.

(CONTINUED)

                          SMOOTH
                    oh you don't trust me?

Breeze just stares at Smooth

                          SMOOTH
                    Come on bro!..

 Mitch and Steve come back in,Steve gives Breeze the thumbs
up.

                          BREEZE
                    so when and where is the drop?

                          SMOOTH
                    2 am..(hands him a note)

Breeze takes the paper,looks at it,puts it in his
pocket,Smooth extends his left fist out to give Breeze a
pound, Breeze looks at Smooths left fist,reaches with his
left hand picks up briefcase,then gives Smooth a pound with
his right fist. Then turns to walk out then stops looks back
at Smooth,they nod at each other,Breeze and Steve leave the
room leaves the room.

Breeze and Steve walking down the hall,Mitch is walking
toward him,Mitch nods at them,but they don't look his way.

Mitch walks back in the room

Breeze and Steve stop and look back down the hall, Breeze
hands the paper to Steve.

                          BREEZE
                    Get some of the boys and go check
                    this out

                          STEVE
                    then who's gonna have your back

                          BREEZE
                    I'll be fine

                          STEVE
                    boss,at least let me-

                          BREEZE
                    Bro,I'm good, you just go make sure
                    everything is straight

                          STEVE
                    So you don't trust Smooth?

                         BREEZE
          The last thing my pops told me
          before he died was never trust
          anyone who comes at you with their
          left hand

                         STEVE
          why is that?

                         BREEZE
          that's the hand you wipe your ass
          with,which means your full of shit!

Steve turns to leave then stops and turns around and pulls
out a gun

                         STEVE
          boss,take it..please

Breeze looks down at the gun,then looks up at Steve.

                                                CUT TO

19 INT-CONFERENCE ROOM- EVENING

Mitch standing by the door,Smooth is sitting down. Smooths
cell phone rings, he answers

                    SMOOTH
          hello

                    BIG UCE
          well?

                    SMOOTH
          it's all set up

Smooth hangs up phone

                                                CUT TO

20 INT- HALLWAY- EVENING

Breeze and Steve walking and talking about to exit building.

                    STEVE
          so where you going to be in the
          meantime?

Breeze looks at his watch

                                                (CONTINUED)

                    BREEZE
I'm a go chill at Katonya's crib

                    STEVE
You want me send some guys over
there to watch your back?

                    BREEZE
Naw,I'll be fine,you just make
sure all is good for tonight!

                    STEVE
I'm on it,I'm stop and get some
lumpia's,then we will be on our way

                    BREEZE
Lumpia's? ,from where?

                    STEVE
Island Breeze Lumpia's,best
lumpia's in town

                                                    CUT TO

21 INT-CONFERENCE ROOM- EVENING

                    MITCH
you think he bought it?

                    SMOOTH
bought what?

                    MITCH
you getting pissed at me,about
Mike?

                    SMOOTH
Don't matter, this time tomorrow..
he'll be dead!

                    MITCH
Boss I been meaning to ask
you..whats up with the what would
Jesus do?

                    SMOOTH
                 (chuckles)
oh that? ,well when my pops got
locked up,I moved in my my
grandfather,he was a preacher,I
respected him,but he was old,and I
was out of control,so he would try
                 (MORE)

                                            (CONTINUED)

                              SMOOTH (cont'd)
                    to play mind games on me, for
                    example,he would go thru my stuff
                    find candy and toys I had
                    stolen,and then at dinner
                    time,would always try to lecture
                    me,talking about the next time you
                    go in a store and you get the
                    notion to steal something,before
                    you reach for it,ask yourself..What
                    would Jesus do?..and then
                    maybe,just maybe, you will do the
                    right thing

                         MITCH
                    So, do you think you did the right
                    thing?

Smooth just sits there with a blank stare,then looks at
Mitch

                                                  FADE TO

22 EXT-APARTMENT COMPLEX- EVENING

Breeze walking to a door, reaches in his pants pocket,pulls
out keys and unlocks and opens door

                                                  CUT TO

23 INT-APARTMENT- EVENING

 He enters house,turns on lights,turns off the alarm, hangs
keys up,heads to the bedroom. He opens the bedroom
door,turns on the light,goes inside bedroom

                                                  CUT TO

24 INT-BEDROOM-EVENING

Breeze enters the bedroom,heads over to a dresser,sits
briefcase down, and begins taking off his jewelry. Bedroom
Bathroom door slowly opens up

Breeze is still at the dresser,he goes to open a drawer and
he is suddenly grabbed from behind by his neck and pulled
back

                                                  CUT TO

25 EXT-WAREHOUSE-EVENING

Steve and 2 of his men outside the warehouse. They enter warehouse from the front.

                                                    CUT TO

26 INT-WAREHOUSE-EVENING

Steve and his men inside the warehouse. They are walking around slowly,inspecting rooms.

1 bodyguard while searching a room is attacked from behind,neck broken by Jace.

1 bodyguard while checking a room,is grabbed from behind and neck sliced by Jace

Steve while searching a room,turns around and Jace is standing in front of him,and Jace pulls out a sword and points it at Steve

                                                    CUT TO

27 INT-CONFERENCE ROOM- EVENING

Smooth and Mitch are in the conference room sitting. Smooth is looking at his watch

                    SMOOTH
              didn't Vince say he would be here
              in 30 minutes!

Mitch nods his head

                    SMOOTH
              call his ass again!

Mitch pulls out his cell phone to call Vince,just as he makes the call,Smooths cell phone goes off

                    SMOOTH
              hello?

                    BIG UCE
              2 down...one to go

Smooth hangs up the phone

                                              (CONTINUED)

                              MITCH
                    got his voice mail again..want me
                    to leave a message?

Smooth slowly shakes his head no

                                                  CUT TO

28 INT-BEDROOM-EVENING

Scan of the bedroom,clothes spread out on the floor,pan up
to the bed and Breeze is in the bed with a female.

They are under the cover kissing,they stop,Breeze rolls over
on his back,female lays her head in his chest. The female is
Katonya,she is a love interest,she thinks he owns a local
club ,unaware of his drug activities.

Katonya is playing with the hairs on his chest

                              KATONYA
                    So when are you going to let me
                    shave your chest?

                              BREEZE
                    right after you shave yours

Katonya hits him,Breeze is laughing

                              KATONYA
                    Fuck you! I aint got no hair on my
                    chest

                              BREEZE
                    oh yeah? whats that right there?

Breeze points to her chest and she looks down,then he raises
his finger up to her lips, and laughs

                              BREEZE
                    gotcha!

Katonya pushes him out of the bed he is laughing at her,gets
up off the floor

                              KATONYA
                    anyway, so can we go to the club
                    tonight?

                              BREEZE
                    naw, not tonight baby,I got to
                    handle some business

                                                  (CONTINUED)

                         KATONYA
                what kind of business?

                         BREEZE
                grown folks business!

Breeze heads to the bathroom and turns on the shower.
Katonya rolls here eyes at him, sits up looks around the room
see's the briefcase on the floor.

                                                        CUT TO

29 INT-KITCHEN- NIGHT

Katonya is in the kitchen, she grabs a knife out of a drawer
and heads over to the table. she has taken the briefcase out
of the bedroom and is trying to pry it open.

                                                        CUT TO

30 INT-BEDROOM-EVENING

Breeze is getting dressed and he looks down where he put the
briefcase and see's its gone

                         BREEZE
                Katonya?

Breeze leaves the bedroom headed to the kitchen

                                                        CUT TO

31 INT-KITCHEN- NIGHT

Katonya reacts to Breeze calling her, she quickly gets up
from the table and goes to the fridge and opens it up.

Breeze walks in wearing a black outfit and his favorite
black fedora hat. See's briefcase on the table, brings slight
smile to his face.

                         KATONYA
                Dam! I need to got to the store

Breeze is checking her out from behind, Katonya shuts the
fridge door and she turns around see's him looking and she
smiles

                    KATONYA
           you like what you see?

                    BREEZE
                  (smiling)
           what do you think

Keisha walks slowly over to him and they kiss.

                    KATONYA
           So are you coming back?

                    BREEZE
           maybe? why you want me to come
           back?

                    KATONYA
           maybe?

Breeze smiles at her winks,grabs the briefcase off the table
and turns to walk out and then the briefcase suddenly opens.
Breeze and Katonya look down on the floor to what has fallen
out of the briefcase. They are both shocked. Katonya walks
over closer to Breeze still looking down at the contents on
the floor.

                    KATONYA
           WHAT THE FUCK ARE YOU REALLY DOING
           TONIGHT!

Katonya looking at Breeze,Breeze still looking at the floor

                    BREEZE
           I'll be dam!

Breeze looks back at Katonya

                    KATONYA
           WELL?

                                                   FADE TO

32 EXT-HALLWAY-NIGHT

Breeze standing in the hallway,thinking,pacing for a
bit,then pulls out his cell phone and dials

                    BREE
           Hey girl, what's good? let me speak
           to D

                                                   CUT TO

33 EXT-BALCONY- NIGHT LAS VEGAS

Man on balcony,woman hands him a cell phone and leaves. Man
is Darnell aka D

> D
> Yo, who dis?

CUT TO

> BREEZE
> Yo D

CUT TO

> D
> what's up B?

CUT TO

> BREEZE
> Bro..listen up..I need a favor

> D
> you want what? mother fucker is you
> high? aint no way in hell-

> BREEZE
> Do what you can brah!

Breeze hangs up the phone,walks to his car

CUT TO

D hanging up phone then dialing making another call

CUT TO

34 INT-RECORDING STUDIO- NIGHT LA

Rap group in studio, laying verses ,then a cell phone rings.

> RAPPER
> Whats' up ?

> D
> yo! check this shit out!

> RAPPER
> get the fuck out of here? when?
> TONIGHT? aint no way in hell!

CUT TO

35 EXT-WAREHOUSE- NIGHT

Breeze is parked outside of the warehouse,sitting in his
car. He gets out scans the area,and heads to the warehouse.
He goes to the front door opens it,and walks inside.

CUT TO

36 INT-WAREHOUSE-NIGHT

Breeze is walking around the warehouse looking in rooms,he
enters one room he see's one of his bodyguards on the
ground. he goes over to check him.

He goes to check another room and see's Steve laying on the
ground in a pool of blood,he goes over to check on him, but
then hears a door open and turns walking toward the sound.

 Jace wearing a mask is creeping around the warehouse
looking for Breeze,and slowly pulls out a samurai sword from
the right side of his body,he hears a noise from a room and
heads slowly to that direction.

Breeze is at a door and and slowly starts to turn the knob.
Jace is outside a door and the knob is slowly turning.
Breeze slowly opens the door. Jace is standing outside as
door slowly opens,and once the door opens all the way,he
quickly jumps in front and swings his sword,and a head is
seen sliced off,head and hat go flying in the air.

FADE TO

37 INT -SMOOTH HOUSE BEDROOM- AFTERNOON

Smooth laying on his bed watching t.v. then he hears someone
knocking at his back door.

Smooth gets up and goes to the door. He opens it,nobody is
there ,he looks left then right,and just as he is about to
shut the door,he looks down and see's a box gift wrapped on
the ground.

He picks the box up,still looking around and then goes back
in the house.

He heads back to his bedroom,holds the box to his ear,to
listen to see if he can hear anything,then he shakes it. He
sits down,starts to take the wrapping off,then opens the
box.

(CONTINUED)

He looks inside the box,slight grin forms on his face,and he pulls out a black fedora hat. He holds it in his hands and studies it for a second,and he knows the hat belongs to Breeze.

A big smile forms on his face and he slowly starts to put the hat on his head

CUT TO

38 INT-KATONYA APT- MORNING

Katonya is sitting on the couch crying,pan to the t.v, there is a news report,with Breeze picture on the t.v.

                    NEWS REPORTER (O S)
               four bodies were found in this
               abandoned warehouse late last
               night,one African American male was
               found decapitated. Police have no
               leads at this time

CUT TO

39 INT-KITCHEN- MORNING

Anastasia is drinking coffee,she is reading a newspaper,turns the page and see's the article about Breeze being killed.

She drops the paper,slumps down on the floor crying

FADE TO

40 EXT-OFFICE BUILDING AFTERNOON

CUT TO

41 INT-OFFICE BUILDING AFTERNOON

Elevator door opens up, Danny and Jace step out of the elevator,they head to the left walk down to the end of the hallway and get to a door, Jace opens it and they both walk in.

CUT TO

42 INT-OFFICE -AFTERNOON

Danny and Jace walk over to desk,and stand in front. Chair
in front of the desk is facing away looking outside the
window at the view.

                    DANNY
             it's all done

Chair slowly turns around and faces Danny and Jace

                    BIG UCE
             show me

Danny turns to the Jace. Jace hands him a box.

Danny places small box on the table.

Big Uce reaches for the box, his chair slowly turns back
around facing the window. He then slowly opens up the
box,and inside the box is a severed finger with a ring on
it. The finger belongs to Breeze.

He takes the finger out the box,takes the ring off the
finger and throws the finger in the trash and puts the ring
on one of his fingers.

Holds his hand out to admire the ring on his finger.

                    BIG UCE
             well done, dismissed

Danny and Jace turn and exit the room

                                        FADE TO

43 INT-OFFICE BLDG-DAY 3 YEARS LATER

Smooth,Mitch and Danny are holding up glasses and they toast
and both drink. They are celebrating their new found
partnership and all the money they have been making.

Danny puts down his glass and hands Smooth a envelope.
Smooth opens it up and pulls out a credit card.

                    SMOOTH
             what is this?

                    DANNY
             See,the days of bags of money are
             over. It' a new era now,from now
             on,all your money will be put in a
                    (MORE)

(CONTINUED)

                         DANNY (cont'd)
          off shore account, accessible by
          that card.

Smooth smiles, they toast and drink again.

Danny looking at Smooth and his clothes that he is wearing
and shakes his head.

                         DANNY
          maybe you should think about
          investing in a new wardrobe?

                         SMOOTH
          whats' wrong with my clothes?

                         DANNY
                    (laughing)
          you look..broke

                         SMOOTH
          that's how we do things, dress like
          regular people, no flossing, that way
          nobody fucks with us,.....that's
          one thing, my boy Breeze taught me

                         DANNY
          well, that was then, this is
          now, nobody is going to fuck with
          you, your connected now!... Besides
          the boss suggested it.

                         SMOOTH
          speaking of the boss, when do I
          finally get to meet him?

                         DANNY
          you don't,...never

                         SMOOTH
          never?

                         DANNY
          put it this way, if you do meet
          him, it means, you fucked up!... and
          you don't want to fuck up!

Danny finishes off his drink, turns and walks out. He then
turns and looks back at Smooth

                         DANNY
          oh and get a better house too!

Danny walks out,shuts the door. Smooth picks up the wine bottle and drinks from it, he holds up the credit card ,looks at Mitch and smiles

                  SMOOTH
        I think it's time to go shopping!

                                    CUT TO

44 EXT-DEALERSHIP- AFTERNOON

Smooth walking around a lot with a car salesman.

He picks out a car he wants. Hands the salesman his credit card.

                                    CUT TO

45 EXT- STREET -AFTERNOON

Smooth driving his brand new car around the town.

Showing off,flossing driving fast all around town.

Eventually pulls up to a big mansion,

                                    CUT TO

46 INT-MANSION-AFTERNOON

Smooth his wife and kids walking around the mansion,wife and kids are excited about the big house.

Smooth and family checking out big family room in the house.

Kids run to check out their bedrooms.

Smooth and his wife go check out their bedroom.

47 INT-HOUSE KITCHEN- AFTERNOON

Woman in kitchen cooking, Her daughter and husband are in the living room watching t.v. The woman is Claire aka Chocolate,while she is cooking her cell phone rings.

                CHOCOLATE
        Hello? I'm on my way

Chocolate hangs up the phone,turns off the pot on the stove
and heads to her bedroom to pack,her husband watches her go
into the room and heads in after her

                                                    CUT TO

48 INT-BEDROOM- AFTERNOON

Chocolate is packing a bag,her husband stands in the doorway
watching her pack

                    TONY
           where are you going?

                    CHOCOLATE
           I'm going to work

                    TONY
           I thought we decided-

                    CHOCOLATE
           No! you decided!

                    TONY
           I don't understand you, you said-

                    CHOCOLATE
           I KNOW WHAT I SAID!

Chocolate stops talking,she see's her daughter standing
behind her husband,looking sad

                    SAMANTHA
           Mommy are you leaving again?

                    CHOCOLATE
           come here pumpkin

Her daughter comes over to her ,looking sad,Chocolate hugs
her.

                    CHOCOLATE
           Mommies has to go to work baby,but
           I'll be back soon, OK?

                    SAMANTHA
           OK?

                    CHOCOLATE
           now you go get ready for dinner

She kisses her daughter and her daughter runs out the room

TONY
I been thinking,maybe I should just
take her-

Chocolate turns and looks at him,with a stern look,points at
him and slowly shakes her head no

CHOCOLATE
don't you ever, you hear me,EVER!

Tony frighten by her look and tone of her voice leaves the
room. Chocolate resumes packing,but packing angrily.

CUT TO

49 EXT-WOODS-AFTERNOON

Soldier hiding behind a tree. He is looking around,a little
nervous holding a rifle in his hands. Looking right then
left, then he slowly begins to move to the right when he is
suddenly attacked from behind,he is grabbed and thrown down
and knife is at his throat. Holding the knife is a female in
tactical gear. This is Pam aka Strawberry.

She leans down and whispers in his ear

STRAWBERRY
your dead!

Another soldier low crawling on the ground,gets to a spot
stops,then slowly crawls a few feet,then gets up and stands
behind a tree.

He scans the area,then turns to head to the right and there
is a rifle pointed right in his face.

Holding the rifle is a female,her name is Angie aka
Vanilla,she is smiling at him and shaking her head

MAN
Dammit!

The soldier and Vanilla start walking and they head to an
open area where there are 3 other soldiers on the ground.
Strawberry is standing in front of them. The soldier with
Vanilla sits down on the ground next to them

Vanilla goes over and stands next to Strawberry

STRAWBERRY
You ladies got a long way to go!
That's all for the day,dismissed!

(CONTINUED)

The men walk away holding their heads down, talking to each other, upset that they got killed by the women.

Strawberry's cell phone rings, she answers

                    STRAWBERRY
          Hello? We are on our way!

She hangs up the phone, turns to Vanilla

                    STRAWBERRY
          Play times over! It's time to go to
          work!

                                              CUT TO

50 EXT-WOODS PARKING LOT- AFTERNOON

Strawberry and Vanilla throw some bags in the back of a jeep and then they get in the jeep, Vanilla starts up the vehicle and speeds off

                                              CUT TO

51 EXT-THUNDERBIRD LOUNGE PARKING LOT- DAY

Point of view of someone walking towards the Thunderbird lounge

                                              CUT TO

52 INT-THUNDERBIRD LOUNGE- DAY

point of view of crowded lounge, walking thru the lounge to the back room, opens door and walks thru, headed to the back corner of the lounge and there is Big L and Lamont sitting in the corner at a table, Waitress serves them drinks, they are smoking cigars and Lamont is telling a funny story, or cracking jokes, after the story, Lamont see's a man walking toward them.

                    LAMONT
          Looks like you got a visitor

Big L looks up and see's a familiar face, Lamont gets up from the table, grabs his drink and leaves

Man walks toward the table, Big L, has a slight smile on his face, the person sits next to him, Big L takes out his lighter and lights it. The person next to him leans in, lighting his cigar

                                         (CONTINUED)

                    BIG L
          The greatest trick the Devil ever
          pulled,was convincing the world he
          didn't exist!

The person leans back and blows smoke up in the air,and its
revealed to be Breeze!

                    BREEZE
          Oh...so I'm the Devil now?

Before Big L can respond waitress come over with his drink.

                    BRENDA
          here you go

Brenda places Big L's drink on table then looks as Breeze

                    BRENDA
          can I get you anything?

Breeze checks out the cute waitress,then smiles at her

                    BREEZE
          let me see, how about,sex on the
          table?

                    BRENDA
               (smiling)
          I think you mean sex on the beach?

                    BREEZE
               (smiling)
          we can do it there too if you like?

Brenda blushing

                    BREEZE
          just a rum and coke baby

Brenda leaves to get the drink, Breeze watches her
leave,checking her out as she walks away

                    BREEZE
          its good to be back home..So what's
          good L?..how's the weed business?

                    BIG L
          its all good..I mean ,I don't make
          as much as I did when I was selling
          bricks,..but at least, nobody is
          trying to kill me!

                         BREEZE
                    oh you got jokes!

Brenda comes over with drink for Breeze

                         BRENDA
                    here's your drink

                         BREEZE
                    thank you

Breeze winks at her,she smiles and leaves

                         BREEZE
                    Thanks for the favor that night

They both raises glasses in the air, they drink,then put
drinks down

                         BIG L
                    So, how did you know it was a set
                    up?

                         BREEZE
                    you remember nosy ass Katonya

                         BIG L
                    yeah

                         BREEZE
                    well I had stopped by her crib to
                    kill some time

                                                    FLASHBACK

53 INT-KITCHEN- NIGHT

Breeze and Katonya look down on the floor to what has fallen
out of the briefcase. They are both shocked. Katonya walks
over closer to Breeze still looking down at the contents on
the floor

                         KATONYA
                    WHAT KIND OF SHIT ARE YOU IN TO!

Katonya looking at Breeze,Breeze still looking at the floor

                         BREEZE
                    I'll be dam!

On the floor,are a bunch of books that has fallen out of the
briefcase. No money

                                                    (CONTINUED)

>   KATONYA
>   What the fuck is going on?
>
>   BREEZE
>   look,I aint got time to explain
>   right now,I'll see you later

Breeze starts picking up the books putting them in the
briefcase. Stands up

>   KATONYA
>   But-
>
>   BREEZE
>   I said later!

Breeze heads to the door, Katonya watches him leave rolls
her eyes

>   BACK TO PRESENT

54 INT-THUNDERBIRD LOUNGE-DAY

>   BIG L
>   So what did you tell her?
>
>   BREEZE
>   Told her to mind her dam business!
>
>   BIG L
>   she did save your life though
>
>   BREEZE
>   true..speaking of saving my life,
>   who was that anyway?

>   FLASHBACK

55 INT-WAREHOUSE-NIGHT

Breeze is seen giving a man his hat and the briefcase.

>   CUT TO PRESENT DAY

56 INT-THUNDERBIRD LOUNGE- DAY

 Breeze Hands Big L a envelope of money

>   (CONTINUED)

                        BIG L
            my brother in law

                        BREEZE
                    (shocked look)
            your brother in law?

                        BIG L
                    (no emotion)
            yep!

                        BREEZE
            you Cold L!

                        BIG L
            it is what it is!

They both take puffs from their cigars

                        BREEZE
            so, you got that spot for me?

Big L pulls some keys a puts them on the table

                        BIG L
            yep,with all the extras!

                        BREEZE
            cool

Breeze picks up the keys and put them in his pocket.

                        BIG L
            so look,I know you about to war,I
            aint got no soldiers, but you can
            use-

                        BREEZE
            there's not going to be any war.
            I'm only going to kill 2
            people,Smooth and the Puppet
            Master!

                        BIG L
            The Puppet Master?

                        BREEZE
            Those hits on me,Vince and
            Mike,were professional! To
            complicated for Smooth to pull off.

                    BIG L
          you sure?

                    BREEZE
          Yeah,I'm sure,he not built like
          that,now if his his old man was
          still around maybe, he was a
          gangster,Smooth got his old man's
          blood,but not his heart!

                    BIG L
          so who you got-

Breeze takes a puff of his cigar,blows smoke out then looks
a Big L and smiles

                    BIG L
          Oh you got your girls!

                    BREEZE
          Dam right!

Breeze starts to get up and leave

                    BIG L
          speaking of your girls, what's up
          with them

                    BREEZE
          what do you mean what's up with
          them?

                    BIG L
          I'm saying,hook me up! I like all 3
          flavors,Chocolate Strawberry and I
          love Vanilla!

                    BREEZE
          Man,they are strictly business!

Breeze sits back down in his chair

                    BREEZE
          oh and Vanilla? Man her last
          boyfriend,she caught him
          cheating,so instead of leaving
          him,the next week,they go to a
          fancy restaurant,go to the
          movies,go back to his crib,and she
          either fucked him and killed him,or
          killed him and fucked him,or was
          fucking him and killing him at the
          same time!

                                        (CONTINUED)

                         BIG L
          Oh Hell No! Forget I asked!

                         BREEZE
          But then again I do owe you a favor
          right? I can hook you up if you
          want?

                         BIG L
          naw I'm good!

                         BREEZE
                    (laughing)
          yeah I thought so

Breeze gets up,give Big L a pound and he starts to walk
out,walks pass the waitress,stops her

                         BREEZE
          Thanks for the drink,keep the
          change (hands her a 100 dollar
          bill)

Brenda see's the bill smiles and gives him a piece of paper

                         BRENDA
          Why thank you,and you keep in touch

Brenda goes over to Big L. Breeze turns and watches her
walk,smiles

                         BREEZE
          Yes!,its good to be home.

Breeze exits

                                                    FADE TO

57 INT-BREEZE HIDEOUT- DAY

Breeze is standing looking out the window, Brenda the
waitress from the Thunderbird hands him a drink. Breeze
takes the drink,sips it.

                         BRENDA
          is there anything else I can get
          you?

Brenda smiling at Breeze,but he is still staring out the
window,then there is a knock at the door

Without looking at her,Breeze answers her

                                               (CONTINUED)

                         BREEZE
              Yeah, get the door,on your way out

Brenda frowns,then goes over to the door,opens it, Chocolate
walks in, Brenda leaves and closes door behind her

Breeze still looking out the window.

                         BREEZE
              Where's the other 2?

                         CHOCOLATE
              There out in the hallway waiting

                         BREEZE
              Waiting?

                         CHOCOLATE
              yeah

                         BREEZE
              waiting for?

                         CHOCOLATE
              We need to talk

Breeze turns and looks at her,Chocolate head down ,not
looking at him

                         BREEZE
              OK let's talk

Breeze opens patio door and heads outside,Chocolate follows
him

                                                  CUT TO

58 EXT-BREEZE HIDE OUT PATIO-DAY

Breeze lights a cigar,Chocolate slowly walks over to him.
Breeze takes a puff from his cigar

                         BREEZE
              Talk

                         CHOCOLATE
              I can't do this anymore

                         BREEZE
              what?

                              CHOCOLATE
                    I , I can't do this anymore

Breeze looks at her

                              BREEZE
                    the fuck you mean you can't do this
                    anymore?

                              CHOCOLATE
                    I can't, I just can't-

                              BREEZE
                    wait hold up? you come out here to
                    tell me this shit to my face? you
                    could have told me this shit on the
                    phone!

                              CHOCOLATE
                    I owed you that much

                              BREEZE
                    no, you owe me a lot more that
                    that!

Chocolate,head down turns and looks away from him.

                              BREEZE
                    all the shit we been thru,I know
                    you not gonna tell me your scared
                    or some bullshit like that!

Chocolate still not facing him,looking away,Breeze walks
closer to her and gets up in her face,looks her up and down

                              BREEZE
                    Naw,you aint scared,its something
                    else,what, you got a conscious all
                    of a sudden,what you trying to get
                    closer to god? what? WHAT IS IT
                    CLAIRE?

                              CHOCOLATE
                    You know what! I AM SCARED! I AM
                    FUCKING SCARED!

                              BREEZE
                    OF WHAT?

Chocolate reaches in her pocket and pulls out a picture of
her daughter and puts it in his face

                                                    (CONTINUED)

                              CHOCOLATE
                    THIS IS WHAT I'M AFRAID OF!

Breeze turns and walks away from her, she starts to follow
him

                              CHOCOLATE
                    Look, shit's changed since I had
                    her, it, it aint in me no more, I got
                    a family now, I want her to-

Breeze raises his hand up and points back to her, as to tell
her to be quiet, he still is not facing her. He looks up
, then closes his eyes , then shakes his head and grins, and
turns to look at Chocolate, then walks over to her

                              BREEZE
                    you know what? if it aint in you
                    , it aint in you

                              CHOCOLATE
                    we straight

                              BREEZE
                    yeah we straight

Breeze extends his right fist to her, she gives him a pound
with her right fist.

Chocolate leaves, Breeze still standing there smoking his
cigar for a while

Vanilla comes out side to where he is

                              BREEZE
                    You know this means more work for
                    you and Strawberry

                              VANILLA
                    we can handle it, but I got
                    question?

Breeze smoking his cigar, looks at her, then looks away

                              VANILLA
                    same price right?

                              BREEZE
                    No, triple!

                              VANILLA
                    triple, shit, lets do this!

Breeze smiles take another puff from his cigar

                                                      (CONTINUED)

                         VANILLA
              oh one more question? so,can I be
              called Chocolate now?

Breeze frowns turns and looks at her,blows smoke in her face
and he heads back inside.

Vanilla coughs and follows behind him

                         VANILLA
              I'm just saying,I like that name
              better and since she not here-

                                                         FADE TO

59 EXT-HOUSE-DAY

Smooth pulls up to a house,parks in the drive way,gets out
the car and heads inside

                                                         CUT TO

60 INT-KITCHEN-DAY

Smooth walking in his house,on his cell phone talking,heads
to his kitchen and goes to the fridge opens it and grabs a
beer,closes the fridge door and turns around and is shocked
when he see's Danny and the Jace standing there

                         DANNY
              I see you took my advice?

                         SMOOTH
              HOW THE FUCK YOU GET INTO MY HOUSE?

Jace begins to walk to Smooth,but Danny stops him

                         SMOOTH
              Oh you want some of this?

                         DANNY
                   (to Jace)
              wait outside

                         SMOOTH
              yeah,get your ass out my house!

Jace slowly walk past Smooth,they both stare each other down
for a second,then Jace smiles,looks back at Danny ,Danny
motions for him to go outside. He leaves

                                                    (CONTINUED)

                    SMOOTH
          This aint cool,I know I work for
          you,but this coming in my house
          shit-

                    DANNY
          My apologies, please sit

                    SMOOTH
          oh you gonna offer me a seat in my
          own dam house?

Danny motions to Smooth to have a seat,Smooth eventually
sits down

                    SMOOTH
          so what can I do for you?

                    DANNY
          we got a shipment coming in from
          the Islands arriving in Oregon in 2
          weeks,passing thru Washington,
          headed to Canada

                    SMOOTH
          How much?

                    DANNY
          about 14 tons

                    SMOOTH
          14 tons?? shit! that's about what
          400-

                    DANNY
          500 million,street value

                    SMOOTH
          500 million? DAM!!

                    DANNY
          now,since the bulk of the shipment
          is going right thru your
          territory,there can be no mistakes!

                    SMOOTH
          you just tell me what you need and
          its done

Danny gets up and heads to the door,then turns around

                              DANNY
                    Oh,if all goes well,you will get
                    10% of the 500,and we will be in
                    control-

                              SMOOTH
                    we already got control? we run this
                    whole fucking state

                              DANNY
                            (laughing)
                    still thinking small,we will
                    control the whole West Coast!

Danny leaves,Smooth sitting on the couch,eyes wide
open,thinking about what he just heard,and its sinking in

                              SMOOTH
                    The whole west coast? HELL YEAH!!!

                                                   CUT TO

61 EXT-SMOOTH HOUSE-DAY

Danny and Jace walk to the drive way get in a car and drive
off

Vehicle on the other side of the street begins to follow,in
the vehicle is Strawberry and vanilla.

                                                   CUT TO

62 INT-BREEZE HIDEOUT-EVE

Breeze and Brenda are culled up on the couch together

                              BRENDA
                    are you hungry?

                              BREEZE
                    naw I'm good

 Strawberry and Vanilla enter the room,they stand for a
second, Breeze motions to Brenda to leave the room.
Strawberry and Vanilla then sit down

                              BREEZE
                    Hope you got some good news

                         STRAWBERRY
          well after tailing your boy for 2
          weeks, we finally got something, he
          had 2 visitors today,they showed up
          at his house an hour before he got
          there,left an hour later.We tailed
          then to this hotel

She hands Breeze a piece of paper

                         BREEZE
          How long they been here?

                         VANILLA
          They checked in last week and due
          to check out the 27th.

                         BREEZE
          umm, so whatever is going down is
          going to happen by then

                         VANILLA
          so what's our next move?

Breeze thinks for a second, gets up ,walks around,then he
smiles and looks at both of them,and they smile

                         STRAWBERRY
          snatch and grab

                         VANILLA
          let's do this

Strawberry and Vanilla turn to leave but Breeze stops them

                         BREEZE
          Hold up,only problem is,the mother
          fucker they working for is
          ruthless,so they might talk so
          easily,or talk at all,so we need a
          back up plan

                                                      CUT TO

63 EXT-HOUSE DAY

Breeze walking up to a house knocks on the door,door opens a
female standing in the door way

                         MAX
          Hello, please come in

64 INT- HOUSE -DAY

Breeze enters the house,Max shuts the door,laying on the couch in front of Breeze is another female Kori,she smiles at him. Max,walks past Breeze and goes and lays next to Kori on the couch.

>   MAX
>   How can we help you today?

>   BREEZE
>   I need to speak to Mama

>   MAX
>   MAMA LA MIA!

>   (OFF SCREEN)
>   OLA

>   MAX
>   this gentleman wants to speak to
>   you

Mama La Mia comes from out of the back,she sees Breeze and smiles and runs over to him and gives him a hug

>   MAMA LA MIA
>   Ola senior Breeze,how you been?

>   BREEZE
>   I been good Mama

>   MAMA LA MIA
>   Papi,you sure? I heard some things?

>   BREEZE
>   Naw Mama,it's cool,I'm taking care
>   of everything, but I do need
>   something from you

>   MAMA LA MIA
>   anything Papi,name it

>   BREEZE
>   I need a woman

Mama La Mia has a shocked look on her face

>   MAMA LA MIA
>   You need a mamasita Papi? Really?

                                        (CONTINUED)

                         BREEZE
                    (laughing)
               oh no Mama,not for me,I need one
               for a job

                         MAMA LA MIA
               awww..OK,well how about one of them

Mama La Mia points to the girls on the couch they both stand
up smiling at Breeze

                         BREEZE
               They are cute,but I need one with
               special talents

                         MAMA LA MIA
               be specific Papi

                         BREEZE
               I need someone to make someone talk
               ,without knowing they talking,you
               know what I mean,like,like-

                         MAMA LA MIA
               Oh like pillow talk?

                         BREEZE
               exactly!

                         MAMA LA MIA
               ummm, I got the perfect girl for
               you...OLA CHURCH!

Mama La Mia points to the upstairs,Breeze looks up and
Church appears,she slowly walks down the steps,looking sexy
and smiling at Breeze. She gets to the bottom of the steps
and goes over and stands right in front of Breeze

                         MAMA LA MIA
               Senior Breeze, Mamasita Church

Church extends her hand out ,Breeze takes her hand and
kisses it. He checks her out .

                         BREEZE
               Church huh? So why do they call you
               that?

Church smiles and walks in front of Breeze then walks behind
him,then leans in and says in his ear

                                              (CONTINUED)

                              CHURCH
                    Because my pussy is so good, I can
                    make the Pope confess!

Breeze is a slightly turned on by what she said,turns to
Mama La Mia

                              BREEZE
                    she will do

                              MAMA LA MIA
                    good,vamonos Church, get your
                    things

Max stands up and walks over to Breeze

                              MAX
                    Hey,I got special talents too?

                              BREEZE
                    Oh yeah,like what?

She pulls out a Sai and twirls it in front of his face

                              MAX
                    PAIN!

Breeze looks at her,walks around her checking her out up and
down,then stops, then looks at Mama La Mia

                              BREEZE
                    I'll take her too

Breeze hands Mama La Mia some money

                                                          CUT TO

65 EXT-STREET-DAY

 A white van parked by the curb,the side door opens up,a man
gets out and grabs a sigh and starts walking up the street
with the sign advertising his comic book,Jace is walking
down the street, he stops to look at the sign the man is
holding.

                              JACE
                    comic book huh? going to be hard to
                    sell,nobody reads anything these
                    days

                              PRESTON
                    Your right,but there is an option
                    for you to purchase the audio
                    version

                                                        CUT TO

66 EXT-STREET ALLEY- DAY

woman on roller skates,helmet,elbow and knee pads,skating
thru the alley,and heads around the corner

                                                        CUT TO

67 EXT-STREET DAY

Preston and Jace are still talking,Jace is walking away from
Preston but he is following trying to convince him to buy
his comic book. Preston eventually steps in front of
Jace,stopping him right by the white van.

                              PRESTON
                    Sir,just hear my 30 second
                    pitch,please?

                              JACE
                    OK you got 30 seconds

Jace looks at his watch,and while Preston is giving his
speech woman on skates is coming up from behind Jace,she
gradually picks up speed,as she gets closer to Jace,Preston
see's her,then moves out of the way,woman on skates lunges
and knocks Jace into the van,she jumps in the van
too,Preston slams the door shut.

                                                        CUT TO

68 INT-VAN-DAY

Jace on the floor of the van rolls over looks up, Strawberry
punches him in the face,knocking him out. Woman on skates
takes off her helmet its Vanilla. Strawberry jumps in the
drivers seat

                                                        CUT TO

69 EXT-STREET- DAY

Van starts up,pulls off. Preston watches van drive off,then
continues walking up the street with his sign.

FADE TO

70 EXT-APARTMENT BUILDING -LATE AFTERNOON

Mitch is in his apt,looking in the fridge taking out food
getting ready to cook,then there is a knock at his door,he
goes the door opens it,standing in the hall way is Church
wearing a silk robe. Mitch is stunned by her beauty and
sexiness

                    CHURCH
          Hi,I don't mean to bother you,but I
          just moved in down stairs,and silly
          me went to take a bath and my hot
          water isn't working. Could I take a
          hot bath in your tub? Please..my
          body is aching?

Mitch eyes wide open is speechless,then get his composure

                    MITCH
          sure come on in,bathroom is this
          way

                    CHURCH
          Thank you

Church walks in takes a few steps inside then turns around
to Mitch

                    CHURCH
          oh,will you come and wash my back
          for me?

Church turns around takes the robe off,it drops to the
floor,and walks to the bathroom,Mitch's has a big smile is
on his face,he shuts the door.

FADE TO

71 INT-ROOM-EVENING

Jace is tied up in a chair,blood coming from his nose and
mouth. Strawberry and Vanilla are standing guard over him.

(CONTINUED)

Breeze enters the room with Max behind him. Breeze walks up
to the Jace pulls up a chair and sits right in front of him
and blows smoke from his cigar in his face.

                    BREEZE
          your gonna tell me everything I
          need to know

Jace spits blood from his mouth on the floor

                    JACE
          or?

                    BREEZE
              (laughing)
          There is no or mother fucker! you
          gonna talk!

                    JACE
          Fuck you and those bitches! I ain't
          telling you shit!

Breeze looks back at the women, he then looks back at
Jace, takes a puff from his cigar, blows the smoke in his face

                    BREEZE
          we will see, ladies he's all yours

Breeze gets up from the chair leaves the room.

Strawberry cracks her knuckles, Vanilla pulls out a big
knife and Max pulls out her Sai's and twirls them and they
all walk toward Jace

                                             CUT TO

72 INT-CONFERENCE ROOM- AFTERNOON

Smooth, Danny are going over the route that the trucks
carrying the dope will be traveling. Mitch is on the phone
calling Church

                    MITCH
          Hey its me again, I left you a
          message earlier, was wondering if
          you want to have dinner later on?
          call me back please

Smooth and Danny are looking at Mitch, Mitch see's them
looking then hangs up the phone

                                        (CONTINUED)

                        MITCH
            sorry boss

Mitch goes over to the table

                        DANNY
            The buses will stop at this truck
            stop,and your drivers will take
            over and get back on the route, and
            take the buses up to the last stop
            before the border,then the
            Canadians will take it from there.

                        SMOOTH
            piece of cake,we got this!

Danny and Smooth shake hands ,Danny leaves.smooth signals
Mitch to come over to him

                        SMOOTH
            I want our best people driving
            those buses!

                        MITCH
            I'm on it boss

Mitch leaves the room,Smooth sits down,looking at the map
and a small grin appears on his face

                                            CUT TO

73 INT-ROOM- EVENING

Breeze walks back in the room, Jace's shirt is off,his face
and chest covered in blood. Strawberry ,Vanilla and Max are
standing beside him,they have blood splatter on them.

Breeze walks over Jace,pushes his head back,he is barely
alive.

                        BREEZE
            Did he talk?

                        VANILLA
            he gave us one name

Vanilla hands Breeze a piece of paper

                        BREEZE
            Danny huh?

Breeze looks at his finger and see's Jace blood on it,then
walks over to Jace and wipes his finger across his chest
then heads over to the wall and begins to write on the wall

Strawberry ,Vanilla and Max all look at him with puzzled
looks on their faces

                    STRAWBERRY
          What the hell are you doing?

                    BREEZE
          I'm leaving a message

Breeze finishes writing on the wall then heads out the
room,Strawberry ,Vanilla and Max follow him,then Vanilla
stops

                    VANILLA
          what about him?

Breeze stops and looks back at Jace

                    BREEZE
          Kill him

Vanilla pulls out her gun and walks over to Jace and shoots
him in the head. They all leave the room.

                                              FADE TO

74 INT-BREEZE HIDEOUT-EVE

Breeze on the phone,Strawberry, Vanilla and Max are relaxing
on the couch.

                    BREEZE
               (on the phone)
          dam girl,you got skills,keep him
          talking baby.

Breeze hangs up phone

                    BREEZE
          Good news,found out they got a
          shipment of coke coming in Thursday
          night,14 tons to be exact

                    STRAWBERRY
          Dam! so what's your plan?

                         BREEZE
          high jack it of course

                         VANILLA
          high jack it? wait a minute, 14
          tons,will be heavily guarded,how
          are we-

                         BREEZE
          hold on,hold on,Oh I didn't mean us

                         STRAWBERRY
          then who?

                         BREEZE
          the feds! see they receive a
          tip,they confiscate the shipment in
          Smooths territory. Putting Smooth
          in a world of shit!

Strawberry and Vanilla both start nodding their heads and
smiling

                         BREEZE
          See one thing I know,we fuck with
          this mans drugs,he will,show his
          face! Then his ass is mine!

                                                       CUT TO

75 INT-SMOOTH HOUSE LIVING ROOM-FRIDAY MORNING

Smooth in his kitchen looking in the fridge, t.v is on,he
hears a news reporter talking,turns up the volume on the t.v

                         NEWS REPORTER
          The largest drug bust in Washington
          history happened late last night.
          Federal agents seized 14 tons of
          cocaine found in this convoy of
          school buses,street value estimate
          about 500 million-

Smooth turns off the t.v,shocked at what he has heard

                         SMOOTH
          What the fuck!

Smooths cell phone rings,he answers

                                                  (CONTINUED)

                          DANNY
                     (on the phone)
                   we need to meet,right now!

Smooth hangs up the phone and starts to dial

                          SMOOTH
                   Mitch! get your ass to the spot
                   right now!

                                              CUT TO

76 INT-CONFERENCE ROOM-AFTERNOON

Smooth ,Danny and Adam another bodyguard, are in the
conference room, Danny is sitting down,Adam standing behind
him,Smooth is pacing back and forth

                          SMOOTH
                   I don't know what happen,but I
                   swear none of my boys talked!

Danny sitting in the chair with Adam behind him,they are
watching Smooth pace back and forth, Mitch comes in the room

                          SMOOTH
                   What the fuck happen last night?

                          MITCH
                   Boss,I ,I ,I don't know

                          SMOOTH
                   The fuck you mean you don't know,I
                   told you to make sure-

Danny slams his hand down on the desk,Smooth and Mitch react
and stop talking

                          DANNY
                   all I know is everything was fine,
                   until the shipment was in your
                   hands!

Danny gets up and walks over to Smooth,Adam follows him

                          DANNY
                   remember when I told you,the only
                   time you would meet the boss is
                   when you fuck up? well,you FUCKED
                   UP! so now-

Danny's phone rings he answers

                                              (CONTINUED)

                              DANNY
                    Hello, what? ...where?

Danny points to his Adam to hand him a pen and piece of
paper on the table. Danny writes down some info

                              DANNY
                    yeah I got it..who the fuck is
                    this?

Danny hangs up the phone, looks at Smooth and Mitch

                              DANNY
                    come with me!

Danny ,Adam,Smooth all leave the room

                                                  CUT TO

77 INT-ROOM-EVENING

Adam slowly opens the door,then enters with his gun drawn.
Danny and Smooth come in behind him. They all look at the
Jace dead body in the chair. Danny walks over to him moves
his head to make sure he is dead.

                              SMOOTH
                    so he must be the one that talked!

                              DANNY
                    No! he didn't know anything about
                    the shipment,so you not off the
                    hook yet!

Mitch has head head down,has a guilty look on his face.

                              DANNY
                    what the fuck does that mean?

Danny pointing to the wall,Smooth and Adam look at what is
written on the wall

on the wall written in blood is

WHAT WOULD JESUS DO?

Smooth immediately knows who has written the message

                              SMOOTH
                    Its BREEZE!

                         DANNY
              who?

                         SMOOTH
              BREEZE!

                         DANNY
              no way we killed him

                         SMOOTH
              are you sure?

                         DANNY
              we don't make mistakes! besides you
              went to his funeral right?

                         SMOOTH
              yeah,but it was a closed casket,and
              his head was cut off remember

                         DANNY
              like I said ,we don't make
              mistakes, must be one of his boys
              we missed

                         SMOOTH
              Naw,anyone that would clap back is
              either dead or locked up

Smooth thinks for a second then takes out his cell phone and
dials

                         SMOOTH
                    (on the phone)
              Yo..I need to know who was close to
              your boy..Breeze who the fuck you
              think I'm talking about!..well you
              better think!....whats her name?

Smooth hangs up the phone

                         SMOOTH
              I'll deal with her myself!

                         DANNY
              Hold up! leave it to the pro's,
              give him the info,call Josue and he
              will take care of it.

                                              CUT TO

78 INT-BREEZE HIDEOUT- DAY

Brenda sitting on the couch,Breeze is outside, smoking,there is a knock on the door. she gets up to answer,opens the door then there is a gun pointed in her face

                                                    CUT TO

79 EXT-BREEZE HIDE OUT PATIO-DAY

Breeze outside smoking a cigar,his cell phone rings

                        BREEZE
             yeah

                                                    CUT TO

                        VANILLA
             Smooth,and the other 3 guys are
             leaving. Who do we follow?

                                                    CUT TO

                        BREEZE
             Don't worry about Smooth,follow the
             other 2,one of them in Danny

Breeze hangs up the phone, still smoking

Then a gun is pointed to the back of his head and the trigger is cocked back.

Breeze smiles ,still smoking ,not fazed by it

                        BREEZE
             I knew you couldn't stay away

Gun is lowered from his head. Breeze turns around and its Chocolate standing in front of him

Chocolate has a slight grin on her face

                                                    CUT TO

80 INT-CONFERENCE ROOM- AFTERNOON

Smooth,pacing back and forth,worried look on his face,takes out his cell and dials

                                                    CUT TO

81 INT-SMOOTHS HOUSE- AFTERNOON

Smooths wife,Donna is at home cooking and their daughters
are sitting in the kitchen, and then her cell phone rings

                        DONNA
              hello,hey-

                                                CUT TO

                        SMOOTH
              listen to me! you need to get the
              girls,and get the fuck out of there
              now!

                                                CUT TO

                        DONNA
              what? I don't under-

                                                CUT TO

                        SMOOTH
              I aint got time to explain,get on a
              plane,go somewhere,anywhere,and
              I'll be in touch

Donna,hangs up her phone.

Donna and kids are grabbing bags.

While kids are packing ,Donna pulls out her cell phone

                        DONNA
              Yes I need a Uber, I'm going to the
              airport

                                                CUT TO

82 INT-MANSION- AFTERNOON

Donna and her daughters are inside the house,Donna nervous
pacing back and forth

                        DONNA
              Hello,we'll be right out!

                                                CUT TO

83 EXT-MANSION- AFTERNOON

Donna and her daughters come running out of the house,they
get into back seat of the vehicle. Driver turns back to look
at Donna

                         DRIVER
                where to?

                         DONNA
                the airport please

Driver turns back around,and its revealed to be Chocolate,
she has a slight grin on her face. car pulls off

                                                  CUT TO

84 INT-BREEZE- HIDEOUT- AFTERNOON

Breeze and Max are playing chess, Brenda brings Breeze a
drink,she then looks over to Max

                         BRENDA
                Can I get you anything?

Max,shakes her head no,concentrating on the chess board,
Brenda walks back over to Breeze and sits on his lap,and
looks at the chess board.

Breeze cell phone rings,he takes it out of his pocket and
answers

                         BREEZE
                what's up

                         VANILLA
                we been following these guys for
                about 2 hours,all around town to
                different spots

                         BREEZE
                you think they made you?

                         VANILLA
                no,my guess is they looking for
                someone,that knows you,since you
                left that message

                         BREEZE
                maybe,but only a few know I'm back,
                and Smooth never met them,so there
                is no way-

                                            (CONTINUED)

                        VANILLA
          wait a minute, here they come,
          another car has pulled up, one got
          in..now the other guy is following
          a female

                        BREEZE
          a female huh,..hold up.. describe
          her?

                                              CUT TO

85 EXT-PARKING LOT-AFTERNOON

Katonya is walking to her car, gets in and pulls off.

Another car begins to follow her

                                              CUT TO

86 INT-BREEZE HIDEOUT-AFTERNOON

Breeze hanging up cell phone,sits back in deep thought for a
second,then moves Brenda off his lap gets up and goes to a
drawer and pulls out a gun then heads running out of the
room.

Max reacts to him leaving grabs her Sai's off the table and
runs after him

                                              CUT TO

87 EXT-PARKING LOT-AFTERNOON

Katonya walking to her apt,with bags in her hand. Get to her
door,pulls out keys unlock door and goes inside

Across the street a car pulls up and its Josue,Jace twin
brother he parks car,gets out and slowly approaches
Katonya's apartment,as he gets to her door,he puts on his
mask

                                              CUT TO

88 INT-KATONYA APT KITCHEN-AFTERNOON

Katonya putting groceries away then heads to her bedroom.

                                          CUT TO

89 INT-KATONYA APT BEDROOM- AFTERNOON

Katonya walks in her bedroom and then is suddenly grabbed
from behind

                                          CUT TO

90 INT-KATONYA APT FRONT DOOR-AFTERNOON

Josue gets the door open and slowly walks in the apartment.
Walking around quietly looking for Katonya. He checks the
bathroom,then he heads to her bedroom

                                          CUT TO

91 INT-BEDROOM-AFTERNOON

Josue slowly walking into the bedroom. Just as he enters and
see's the bed he hears a whistle then looks to the right and
is hit in the face by a masked man,the masked man is holding
Katonya too.

Josue falls down and when he starts to get up Max comes from
out of the other bathroom with a gun drawn pointed at Josue
on the floor. Josue slowly sits back down and puts his hands
up.

Mask man pushes Katonya on the bed,points to her to sit
there.

                    MASKED MAN
                 (to Katonya)
             Don't move

                    MASKED MAN
                 (to Max)
             put him the van

Max motions to Josue to get up,he gets up, Mask man stops
him and takes off his mask. Max and Mask man look at each
other and realize that he looks like the the man they
tortured and killed earlier.

                                          (CONTINUED)

                        MASK MAN
            Twins huh?. Put his as in the van!

Katonya looking at Mask man,she kind of recognizes his
voice. Mask man begins to walk out,then stops and turns
around and walks toward her,

Katonya is scared and starts to back away. Mask man begins
to slowly take off his mask, and reveals his face to her.
Its Breeze

Katonya,shocked look on her face jumps up and goes to hug
him

                        KATONYA
            OH MY GOD! OH MY GOD! your alive!
            Your alive!

Katonya is squeezing and hugging him tight,then her
happiness turns to anger

                        KATONYA
            YOU SON OF A BITCH!

Katonya punches Breeze in the face,he falls back against the
wall, Max runs back in with her gun drawn pointed at
Katonya. Breeze waves at Max to back off,she leaves the room

Breeze holding his jaw

                        BREEZE
            Good to see you too baby

                        KATONYA
            I DON'T FUCKING BELIEVE THIS SHIT!

                        BREEZE
             Look just sit down and let me
            explain

Katonya stands for a second ,still pissed off then comes
over and sits next to Breeze

                        BREEZE
            Now let me explain

                                              CUT TO

92 INT-KITCHEN-AFTERNOON

Max looking in the fridge for food .

                                                    CUT TO

93 INT-BEDROOM-AFTERNOON

Breeze and Katonya on the bed, he is explaining everything
to her

Katonya is shocked by all the information she has heard.

                         KATONYA
                A fucking drug dealer? really? I
                thought you worked at the club?

                         BREEZE
                well,actually I own the club,and
                this apartment complex, which
                reminds me, I'm raising your rent

Katonya looks back at him with a mean look on her face

Breeze nudges her

                         BREEZE
                its a joke

Katonya rolls her eyes and looks away from him

                         BREEZE
                look ,I'm sorry I had to lie to
                you,but I did it for your own good
                to keep you safe

                         KATONYA
                umm,Hello! didn't someone just try
                to kill me?

                                                    CUT TO

94 INT-LIVING ROOM AFTERNOON

Max walking around apartment checking things out, puts the
gun down on the table,takes out her Sai's starts to twirl
them around.

                                                    CUT TO

95 INT-BEDROOM-AFTERNOON

Breeze and Katonya still on bed talking

                    KATONYA
          so your brother's getting killed in
          the war,that was a lie too?

                    BREEZE
          no,they were killed in the war,just
          not the war you thinking about

                    KATONYA
          so why all the lies? what you don't
          trust me?

                    BREEZE
          its not that,see growing up, with
          my Mom,going to see my dad once a
          week for 15 years,communicating
          through that glass, not being able
          to touch him, watching him die
          slowly,then my brothers getting
          killed. I told myself,if I was
          going to be in the game,I was going
          to do it alone, No wife,no kids,
          just only worry about myself. The
          shit my Mom went through,I don't
          wish that on anyone. She died a
          broken heart.

Katonya reaches for his hand to console him

                    KATONYA
          So you saying you have no feelings
          at all?

Breeze slowly turns and looks at her

                    BREEZE
          look I aint no monster,Im human,I
          mean I got desires,and needs,but
          love is not one of them,Love clouds
          your mind,makes you do dumb shit.

                    KATONYA
          How you figure that?

                    BREEZE
          I'll give you a perfect example, If
          Adam didn't love Eve,he would have
          never bitten the apple

Breeze cell phone rings he answers

(CONTINUED)

                              BREEZE
                    Yeah, we got him, just stay on the
                    other one

Breeze hangs up the phone

                              KATONYA
                         (sarcastic)
                    so that bitch out there? she takes
                    care of your needs?

                              BREEZE
                    no, that's business, I never mix
                    business with pleasure, pack your
                    shit, let's go

Breeze gets up and heads for the door, Katonya picks up the
gun Josue dropped on the floor, and cocks the hammer and aims
the gun at Breeze.

Breeze hears the trigger cocked and turns around to face her

                              KATONYA
                    well look here mister big time drug
                    dealer, what am I? business or
                    pleasure, if I'm business, then I
                    want to get paid, and if I'm
                    pleasure, (smiles) then I want to
                    get laid!

Breeze looks at her and a slight smile comes across his
face, and he shakes his head

                                                        CUT TO

96 EXT-PARKING LOT-AFTERNOON

Breeze is hugging Katonya, Max is standing by next to
them, looking around

                              KATONYA
                    Will I ever see you again?

Breeze shakes his head no, then hands her some money, she
slowly takes it hugs him again, and gets in the car.

Max walks over to Breeze

                              BREEZE
                    Make sure she gets on the
                    plane, then head back to the spot.

                                                        (CONTINUED)

                                    MAX
                    what about him?

                                    BREEZE
                    I got something special planned for
                    him

                                            FADE TO

97 EXT-PARK-NIGHT

Breeze is standing over Josue,he is tied up,on his knees
beaten, Breeze is walking around him slowly in a circle

                                    JOSUE
                    That's everything I know, I swear!

Breeze walks around him one more time,then stops right in
front of him

                                    BREEZE
                    I told you,if you talked,I wouldn't
                    shoot you in the head,like I did
                    your brother!

Josue,looking at Breeze huffing and puffing

Breeze pulls out a cigar and lights it.

Breeze then looks around ans shrugs his shoulders like he is
cold

                                    BREEZE
                    its a little chilly out here, yo,
                    you cold? you want a blanket or
                    something?

Josue just stars a Breeze

                                    BREEZE
                    Yo my man, give him something to
                    keep him warm

Man steps forward, Josue eyes gets real big,he screams, man
is a fire breather and sets Josue on fire.

Breeze watches him burn to death,then walks away

                                            FADE TO

98 INT-SMOOTH MANSION-MORNING

Smooth staring out of his window in deep thought

CUT TO

99 INT-SMOOTH MANSION BEDROOM- MORNING

Smooth packing some bags of clothes and money grabs his gun
loads it and puts in his shoulder holster . Takes out his
cell phone,makes a call

                SMOOTH
        Mitch, we got to get the fuck out
        of here,meet me at the hanger in an
        hour.

Smooth hangs up the phone and heads to the front door

CUT TO

100 EXT-MANSION FRONT DOOR-MORNING

Smooth leaving his house,exits out the front door,takes a
few steps then is kicked in the face by Chocolate and
knocked out .

FADE TO

101 EXT-MITCH APT-MORNING

Mitch running to his apartment,opens the door and heads
inside.

CUT TO

102 INT-MITCH APT-MORNING

Mitch inside his apartment,calling for Church

                MITCH
        Hey baby where you at?

                CHURCH
        I'm in the bed baby,come join me

Mitch runs to the bedroom

CUT TO

103 INT-MITCH BEDROOM-MORNING

Mitch inside his bedroom,see's Church still in bed under the covers,he starts getting clothes out of his closet

                    MITCH
          Baby,you got to get up and get
          dressed,we got to go

Church in the bed,just moves around a bit,but does not get up

Mitch still getting stuff out of the closet,looks back at her then goes over to the bed,and nudges her

                    MITCH
          baby,come on we got to go!

Church still does not move,then Mitch pulls back the covers and is shocked when he see's it's Breeze laying in the bed,and Breeze has a gun pointed at Mitch and fires instantly!

Mitch falls back against the wall,Breeze gets up out of the bed, Church gets up off the floor from the other side of the bed.

Church and Breeze both walk over and stand by Mitch and watch him take his last breath before Breeze shoots him again.

Breeze then pulls out some money and hands it to Church

                    BREEZE
          Job well done

                    CHURCH
          my pleasure

Breeze and Church leave the bedroom

                                        CUT TO

104 INT-MITCH FRONT DOOR-MORNING

Breeze and Church are about to leave when Church suddenly stops and turns to Breeze

                    CHURCH
          oh,I almost forgot

Church pulls out a piece of paper and hands it to Breeze,he opens it up

                                        (CONTINUED)

                         BREEZE
              MOTHER FUCKER!

                                                          CUT TO

105 INT-BREEZE HIDEOUT-AFTERNOON

Strawberry,Vanilla are sitting at the table. Breeze and
Chocolate are outside talking

                                                          CUT TO

106 EXT-BREEZE HIDEOUT-AFTERNOON

Breeze smoking a cigar,Chocolate standing next to him

                         BREEZE
              Smooth?

                         CHOCOLATE
              He is on ice, and that girl Max, is
              with him...what about his wife and
              kids?

Breeze turns and looks at Chocolate for a second, then looks
away takes a long puff from his cigar,blows the smoke in the
air

                         BREEZE
              Put them on a plane

                         CHOCOLATE
              you sure?

                         BREEZE
              yeah

Chocolate leaves, Breeze watches her walk away, tosses his
cigar,Vanilla comes up beside him watching Chocolate leave

                         VANILLA
              What now?

                         BREEZE
              we end this shit!

                                                          CUT TO

107 INT-SMOOTH BEDROOM-AFTERNOON

Smooth handcuffed to his bed,mouth taped shut,still knocked out,Max siting in a chair reading a magazine. Smooth slowly opens his eyes and starts to struggle to try and break loose,Max still reading the magazine ignoring what he is doing.

Smooth stops struggling and hears footsteps approaching his bedroom door.

Bedroom door opens up,and Strawberry and Vanilla walk in and stand at the foot of the bed. Smooth eyes get bigger,then he hears some more footsteps and Breeze slowly walks in the room,Smooths eyes get bigger as he see's Breeze.

Breeze not looking at Smooth,he walks past Strawberry and Vanilla, Max gets up out of the chair,and Breeze sits down in the chair,then he finally looks at Smooth.

Smooth breathing heavily,scared to death.

Breeze just sits and stares at him for a moment.

                    BREEZE
          What's up Bro? Long time no see!
          How you been?

Smooth still huffing and puffing,Breeze looking around the room

                    BREEZE
          Nice house by the way

Breeze sits up and leans toward Smooth

                    BREEZE
          So before you die, and oh don't get
          it twisted,your going to die, there
          is just one question I want to
          ask,... is why the FUCK,didn't you
          reach out to us,and say hey, this
          mother fucker stepped to me,
          threatened me! threatened all of
          us! and we need to handle this
          shit! Wasn't that the main reason
          for forming the ALLIANCE! ...WELL??

Breeze then signals to Vanilla to take the tape off of Smooths mouth,she walks over and yanks it off.

                                        (CONTINUED)

> SMOOTH
> Man,I,I didn't know,I didn't know
> what was going on,and when I
> finally found out,it was too late,I
> wanted to strike back,but I was
> cornered!

> BREEZE
> Like you are right now huh?

> SMOOTH
> Bro,the gun was pointed at my
> head,dude gave me choice, live of
> die? So I choose to live, what
> would you do?

Breeze sitting back in the chair looking up at the ceiling
then gets up out of the chair

> BREEZE
> See if it was me? I would have
> called his bluff,and looked him in
> dead in his eyes, and tell him to
> pull the mother fucking trigger!
> But that's me

Breeze slowly walking toward the head of the bed, Smooth
huffing and puffing getting scared

> SMOOTH
> Man,we can still get him,I,I know
> where to find him!

> BREEZE
> (laughing)
> On now you want to team up! Now you
> want to fight back! (looking at the
> girls) can you believe this some
> shit!

Breeze looking at Smooth,holds out his right hand and
Strawberry takes out a gun and hands it to Breeze, Breeze
grabs the gun,never taking his eyes off of Smooth,staring
him dead in the face.

Breeze with the gun in his right hand slowly lowers his
hands down and crosses them together in front of his waist.

He slowly shakes his head at Smooth, Smooth tearing up
sensing he is about to die.

(CONTINUED)

                    BREEZE
          That day,when you were asked, if
          you wanted to be a rich man,or a
          dead man, did you ever ask
          yourself, what would Jesus do?

Smooth looks around,closes his eyes,shakes his head slowly

                    SMOOTH
          No, I didn't

                    BREEZE
          Well,..when you see him, you can
          ask him!

Breeze,Strawberry and Vanilla fire their weapons killing
Smooth.

They all head out of the bedroom,Breeze stops before leaving
the bedroom,opens the closet and grabs his Black fedora hat,
slowly puts it on his head

                                                   CUT TO

108 INT-MANSION HALLWAY-AFTERNOON

Strawberry,Vanilla and Max in the hallway,Breeze is heard
coming down the stairs,he meets them in the hallway

                    BREEZE
                 (to Strawberry)
          We still got a few hours,you know
          what to do

Strawberry nods and leaves. Breeze takes a piece of paper
out of his pocket and hands it to Vanilla

                    BREEZE
          Go take care of Danny

                    VANILLA
          what about that other thing?

                    BREEZE
          I'll take care of it myself

Vanilla leaves,Breeze looks at his watch,then turns to Max

                    BREEZE
          Hey,you hungry?

                         MAX
          I'm starving!

                         BREEZE
          you like Lumpia?

                         MAX
            yeah

                         BREEZE
          I know place that makes the best
          lumpia's in town

                                                    CUT TO

109 INT-SALON EDWARDS-EVENING

Barber is giving a customer a hair cut in the first chair. 2
other chairs are empty, towards the back of the barber
shop,there are 3 men.2 bodyguards and Big Uce. In the rear
of the barbershop there is a woman underneath the hairdryer.
Big Uce is reading a newspaper.

One of the bodyguards looks at his watch, The the front door
to the barbershop opens. It's Breeze and Max.

                         BREEZE
          I have a order from Island Breeze
          Lumpia's

One bodyguards gets up and pulls his guns out pointing them
at Breeze and Max.

Big Uce motions to the other bodyguard to have them come
over. Bodyguard points to Breeze and tells him to come.
Breeze and Max slowly walk toward the back of the
barbershop.

As they get close to the back,bodyguards stops them and pats
them down, and checks the bags of food.

                         BODYGUARD
            Their clean

Big Uce motions him to have Breeze come over. Bodyguard
points to Breeze to go.

Breeze motions to Max to give the bodyguard on the right
some food,Breeze takes the other container of food and goes
over to Big Uce

                                              (CONTINUED)

                              BREEZE
                    May I?

Big Uce continues reading his paper and does not acknowledge
Breeze.

                              BREEZE
                    I'll take that as a yes

Breeze sits down next to Big Uce and opens container of
lumpia's ,and puts container in front of him,offering him
some

                              BREEZE
                    compliments of Island Breeze
                    catering

Big Uce looks at food then looks at Breeze

Breeze smiles and picks up a lumpia and eats it. looking
dead into Big Uce's face,then offers one to Max and she eats
one too.

Then puts the container back in front of the Big Uce,Big Uce
motions to his bodyguard on his left. He takes the container
and starts eating them,and the bodyguard on the right starts
eating his food.

Big Uce still reading his paper begins to talk to Breeze,but
never looking at him,as he is turning pages,Breeze notices
his ring on the right hand of Big Uce.

                              BIG UCE
                        (in Samoan language)
                    who are you? and what do you want

                              BODYGUARD
                    he said who are you and what do you
                    want?

                              BREEZE
                    who I am is not the question,the
                    question is,How do I know you!

Barber stops cutting customers hair,and looks to the back

Both bodyguards stop eating and look over at Breeze and Big
Uce.

Big Uce stops turning pages,and turns and looks at
Breeze,they stare at each other for a few seconds,then Big
Uce slowly turns back to reading his newspaper.

                                                      (CONTINUED)

Bodyguards resume eating their food,barber goes back to cutting hair.

                    BIG UCE
                 (in Samoan)
          say what you came here to say

                    BODYGUARD
          say what you came here to say?

                     BREEZE
          you do speak English right?

Big Uce looks at Breeze and frowns

                     BREEZE
          I'll make this quick,your
          partner,or shall I say former
          partner Smooth,has taken a leave of
          absence

                     BIG UCE
          So,you want to be his replacement
          huh?

                     BREEZE
          No!,I'm nobodies pawn,

Breeze then looks at Bodyguard

                     BREEZE
          or flunky!,and speaking of
          flunkies,where is yours?

Big Uce Looks at Breeze,then at his Bodyguard then nods at him. Bodyguard takes out his cell phone and starts to dial

                                              CUT TO

110 EXT-PARKING LOT-AFTERNOON

Danny walking to his car. Gets in,he puts key in the ignition,then Vanilla appears from the back seat,grabs Danny's head ,pulls it back and slices his throat.

Vanilla gets out of the car and walks away.

Danny's cell phone begins to ring.

                                              CUT TO

111 INT-SALON EDWARDS-EVENING

                    BREEZE
          So which one of you clowns is Big
          Uce?

Bodyguard looks at Breeze and gets up walks toward Breeze
and stands over him.

                    BODYGUARD
          Hey! you better watch your mouth!
          and show some respect, boy!

Breeze slowly takes off his hat and stands up and gets right
in the bodyguards face.

                    BREEZE
          Don't let my smile,good looks and
          cloths fool you big boy, I'll put
          something on your ass!

Breeze and Bodyguard stare at each other for a moment. The
Big Uce tells the Bodyguard to sit down

                    BIG UCE
               (in Samoan)
          go sit back down and eat your food

Bodyguard goes and sits back down and eats his food. Breeze
sits back down next to Big Uce

                    BIG UCE
          Say what you came to say and make
          it quick,boy!

                    BREEZE
          Boy!(chuckles to himself) Here's
          the deal,shit is going back to the
          way it use to be, the good ole
          days,you can have all the other
          territories,but I'm taking back the
          South!

Big Uce looks Breeze up and down and laughs

                    BIG UCE
               (in Samoan to bodyguard)
          Check out the balls on this nigger!

Both Bodyguards laughs. Breeze looking at all of them
laughing,waits for them to stop.

Breeze then leans in closer to Big Uce

(CONTINUED)

> BREEZE
> Oh,and any thoughts of you ever
> coming down south,or stepping to
> me? best remain a thought!

Bodyguards stop eating and stand up,Barber stops cutting
hair. Big Uce slowly lowers his newspaper,then turns and
faces Breeze,and looks Breeze dead in his face

> BIG UCE
> Is that an order? or a threat?
> because I don't take any from
> Niggers!

Breeze and Big Uce stare at each other for a second, Breeze
then grins the slowly stands up

> BREEZE
> Enjoy your lunch

Breeze walks away from Big Uce, looks in the mirror puts on
his hat,adjusts it then turns to walk out,Max follows behind
him.

Bodyguard watches Breeze and Max, Breeze stops to talk to
the barber, Big Uce goes back to reading his paper.

> BREEZE
> (to Barber)
> Hey how much for a fade and to line
> me up

Back of the barbershop,the woman under the hairdryer gets up
and pulls out 2 guns, its Strawberry,she fires and shoots
Both Bodyguards in their heads and the turns and points gun
at Big Uce shooting him in the head.

Breeze walks to the back and goes over to Big Uce and takes
his ring off his finger and puts it on his finger.

Breeze, Max and Strawberry then head to the front door,but
then Breeze stops and turns to look for the barber who is on
the floor behind his chair,scared

> BREEZE
> Yo, How much for a fade and line
> up?

> BARBER
> (stuttering)
> tttw,tttw„tttw,twennnn,twenty five

Breeze laughing at him

(CONTINUED)

                              BREEZE
                    you got a card?

Barber points to the counter, Breeze grabs a card,then
leaves.

                                                         CUT TO

112 EXT-SALON EDWARDS-EVENING

Breeze,Max and Strawberry are standing outside, Max pulls
out the cigar with the ribbon on it

                         STRAWBERRY
                    ready for your victory cigar?

                         BREEZE
                    not yet,one more thing to take care
                    of

                                                         CUT TO

113 EXT-APT-AFTERNOON

Church walking in the hallway gets to Knocking on the door

                                                         CUT TO

114 INT-APT-AFTERNOON

Steve on the couch watching T.V, hears knock at the door and
goes to answer

                                                         CUT TO

115 EXT-APT HALLWAY-AFTERNOON

Church holding a bag of food

                         CHURCH
                    I got your order from Island Breeze
                    Lumpia?

                         STEVE
                    Bout time

Steve turns around to grab his wallet and when he turns back
around Breeze is in the doorway with gun drawn, and shoots
Steve in the head.

                                                    (CONTINUED)

Steve falls to the ground. Breeze walks in and stands over him,looking at Steve's face,Steve dead,eyes wide open,with surprised look on his face

FADE TO

116 EXT-BREEZE HIDEOUT-AFTERNOON

Breeze hugging Strawberry and Vanilla and giving them money for a job well done.

Strawberry and Vanilla leave, Brenda comes over to Breeze and gives him the big cigar.

Breeze takes the red ribbon off the cigar, Brenda pulls out the cutter,cuts the cigar for Breeze.

Breeze puts the cigar in his mouth, Brenda pulls out a lighter, Breeze leans in puffs on cigar

CUT TO

117 EXT-BOAT-EVENING

Breeze puffing on the cigar,getting it lit,then leans back,he is on the deck of a boat, Brenda is sitting next to him and a few other girls in bikini's are on the boat.

Breeze enjoying the view of the lovely ladies and the water,and they sail away

FADE OUT

THE END

END CREDITS

Made in the USA
Middletown, DE
01 August 2019